TEDD ARNOLD

HUGGLY'S®
TRIP TO THE BEACH

SCHOLASTIC INC.
Cartwheel B·O·O·K·S®

New York   Toronto   London   Auckland   Sydney
Mexico City   New Delhi   Hong Kong   Buenos Aires

P9-BXZ-156

For the Florida girls—
Mary, Louise, Linda, Carol,
Jeanie, Bobbie, and Lanita
— T. A.

No part of this publication may be reproduced, or stored in a retrieval system, or transmitted in any form or by any means, electronic, mechanical, photocopying, recording, or otherwise, without written permission of the publisher. For information regarding permission, write to Scholastic Inc., Attention: Permissions Department, 555 Broadway, New York, NY 10012.

Copyright © 2002 by Tedd Arnold.
All rights reserved. Published by Scholastic Inc.
HUGGLY and THE MONSTER UNDER THE BED are trademarks and/or registered trademarks of Tedd Arnold.
SCHOLASTIC, CARTWHEEL BOOKS, and associated logos are trademarks and/or registered trademarks of Scholastic Inc.

Library of Congress Cataloging-in-Publication Data available

ISBN 0-439-32448-3

12 11 10 9 8 7 6 5 4 3   02 03 04 05 06

Printed in the U.S.A.
First printing, April 2002

"Where are we?" asked Huggly.

Booter, Grubble, and Huggly were on an expedition.
With snacks in their packs and a star crystal for exploring
dark tunnels, they had set off from their own Secret Slime
Pit to look for new and bigger slime pits.

"Well," said Booter, "according to this, we just went off the map."

"I'm hungry," said Grubble, pulling off his snack pack.

"We should probably turn around now," Booter suggested.

"Wait," said Huggly. "We haven't found any really big slime pits yet. I just want to peek around one more corner."

"W-w-w-wow!"
said Huggly.
    Booter and Grubble
hurried to take a look.

Hatchways lined the ceiling of a long, straight tunnel that stretched as far as they could see. They knew, of course, that hatchways always opened under people beds.

"That's a lot of beds," Huggly whispered. "What kind of people place is up there?"

"I suppose we could explore it before we turn around," said Booter.

They dropped the star crystal and their snack packs. Each of them picked a different hatchway and climbed up the steps.

Huggly peeked out from under a bed. The room was quiet, so he decided to look around. He had never seen a bedroom quite like this before. It was too clean, not at all like the people child's bedroom where he always played.

There was the biggest
bed he had ever seen.

There was a glass box that
started talking and laughing
when he pushed a button.

There was an empty slime pit.
When Huggly turned a handle it
started squirting water all over
the place.

Huggly saw a door he hadn't tried yet. Carefully, he pulled it open and stepped out into a long, quiet people tunnel.

Just then, Booter and Grubble came out of the rooms they had been exploring.

"Hey, guys! Wait 'til you see the stuff I found!" said Huggly.

"First, you have to see what I found," said Booter.

"No! Me first," Grubble insisted.

Suddenly they heard the doors click shut behind each of them.

"Umph! I can't get this open," Booter muttered.

"We're locked out!" cried Grubble.

"We have to find some other bed to get under," said Huggly.

They tiptoed along the tunnel, afraid that some people might catch them. Beside a pair of doors that had no knobs, Huggly saw two buttons. He pushed one and it lit up.

"Must you push every button you see?" asked Booter.

"I love pushing buttons," said Huggly.

Suddenly the doors slid open. They stepped into a little room.

"It's empty," said Grubble. "No bed. No nothing!"

"Except these buttons," said Huggly. He gleefully pushed them until they were all lit up.

The doors without handles slid shut.
Then the room started to move.
"We're trapped!" Grubble yelled.

"We're going up," said Booter. Soon the room jolted, then stopped. All three monsters held their breath as the doors slid open.

"I'm outta here!" cried Grubble.

"Me, too!" said Huggly.

"Wait for me!" said Booter.

The three friends found themselves at the end of another long tunnel. This tunnel looked exactly the same as the last one except there were some people things left behind.

They found some snacks.

There was a tiny
slime pit on wheels . . .

and a big cart
of some kind.

Just then a people person came out of a nearby door. Quickly, Huggly, Booter, and Grubble hid inside the cart underneath some pieces of white cloth. The people person pushed the cart down the tunnel toward the little moving room.

The doors slid open, the cart was pushed into the little room, and the doors closed.

The monsters could feel themselves going down, down, way down.

Huggly, Booter, and Grubble felt a thump and heard the doors open. The people person pushed the cart out into a big, noisy place. Then she stepped back into the little room. The doors shut and the monsters were alone again.

"I don't see any beds here," Grubble muttered.

"Let's find a way out," said Booter.

"But first," said Huggly, "we should disguise ourselves in this white stuff. That people person almost caught us!"

Once they had covered themselves, they hurried to a
couple of big doors with handles and opened them.
Huggly and his friends took a look outside.

The sunlight was very bright. The black ground was
so hot on their feet that they all cried out, "Ouch! Ooie!
Ouch!"

At last they jumped into some shady plants to hide.
They looked back at where they had come from. It was the
tallest people house they had ever seen.

"What's that roaring noise?" asked Huggly.
They turned around to look.
"Whoa!" said Grubble. "That's the biggest
slime pit I've ever seen!"

They ran through soft, white stuff to the edge of the huge slime pit and cooled their feet.

"Let's dive in!" said Huggly.

"We can't," warned Booter. "We might lose our disguises."

Instead, Huggly collected pretty things he found at the edge of the slime.

Grubble looked for snacks.

Booter built her own little slime pit.

"Oh, wow!" said Huggly. "I see a monster just like us and it isn't even hiding."

"That's not possible," said Booter. But Huggly ran off so quickly, he didn't hear what she said. And he didn't realize that his friends weren't following him.

Huggly walked up to the monster and said,
"Hi!" It didn't answer. He patted the tail and it
bounced lightly.

"Oh," said Huggly to himself. "You're just
a people toy."

He saw a button on its side and pushed it. Air whooshed out of the monster and it slowly fell flat.

"Oops!" said Huggly. "I broke it!"

He took a piece of cloth from his back and covered the flattened toy with it.

Suddenly a strong gust of wind blew away the rest
of Huggly's disguise.

At that moment, a dripping wet people child rushed
up from the big slime pit. "Now I'm going to ride my
monster floatie!" he announced. He grabbed Huggly and
dragged him into the slime.

Finally a big wave of slime tumbled Huggly and the people child onto the white stuff. In a flash, Booter and Grubble raced over, grabbed Huggly, and ran away.

The people child cried, "They took my floatie!"

"No, dear," said his mother. "You must have had *their* floatie. I have yours right here. I just blew it up."

It took a lot of sneaking, but Huggly, Booter, and Grubble made their way back into the tall people house.

It took a lot of waiting before they spotted a door left open for just a moment.

It took a lot of scrambling to get past the people person in the room and dive under a bed without getting caught.

Once back in the monster world, they found
their star crystal and snack packs right where they
had left them.

"Now what?" asked Grubble.

"Back home?" asked Booter.

"Yeah, I'm tired," said Huggly. "And anyway,
it will be nice to be back at our own slime pit. It's
just the right size."